The Quiet F

A scurvy tale of derring-do

On his ninetieth birthday, Admiral Obadiah Barrett (retired) summoned his only living relative to his bedside.

'Great nephew,' croaked the old man, 'you've been a disappointment to me these last forty years. A great disappointment . . . The Barretts have always been sea-going men, men of derring-do. But you . . . what are you again?'

'Er, Pea - Counter - in - Chief to King Garry and Queen Dawn,' confessed William Barrett.

'Stap me vitals!' boiled the Admiral. 'Pea-counting is no occupation for a Barrett! But it may not be too late for you yet . . .'

Also by Andrew Matthews

Wolf Pie
Dixie's Demon

ANDREW MATTHEWS

The Quiet Pirate
A scurvy tale of derring-do

Illustrated by Tony Ross

MAMMOTH

For my godchildren:
Simon, Jessica, Ben, Tom and Jonathan.

A Mammoth Paperback

THE QUIET PIRATE

First published in Great Britain 1988
by Methuen Children's Books
Paperback edition published 1989 by Mammoth
an imprint of Mandarin Paperbacks
Michelin House, 81 Fulham Road, London SW3 6RB

Text copyright © 1988 Andrew Matthews
Illustrations copyright © 1988 Tony Ross

ISBN 0 7497 0041 6

A CIP catalogue record for this title is available
from the British Library

Printed in Great Britain
by Cox & Wyman Ltd, Reading

Contents

One: Go to the port of Littlewick

On his ninetieth birthday, Admiral Obadiah Barrett (retired) summoned his only living relative to his bedside.

Admiral Barrett had a bony face with a great hooked nose and as he sat in bed, propped up with pillows, wreathed in coils of evil-smelling smoke from a long clay pipe, he resembled an osprey perched on a misty crag.

'Great nephew,' croaked the old man, 'you've been a disappointment to me these last forty years. A great disappointment.' He pointed with a claw-like finger to a row of paintings hanging beside his bed, all portraits of beefy-looking men in sailor uniforms. 'The Barretts have always been sea-going men, men of derring-do. But you . . .' Old Obadiah's bristly white eyebrows gathered into a puzzled frown. 'What are you again?'

'Er, Pea-Counter-in-Chief to King Garry and

Queen Dawn,' confessed William Barrett.

'What the blazes is a pea-counter?' snapped old Obadiah.

'Well,' explained William nervously, 'a pea-counter is a man who counts peas. You see, long ago, King Damien the Bad-Tempered decreed that all the peas in the kingdom of Dunroamin must be counted and graded annually.'

'Why?' demanded Obadiah.

'No one knows,' blushed William. 'King Damien was so bad-tempered that nobody dared to ask him . . .'

'Stap me vitals!' boiled the Admiral. 'Pea-counting is no occupation for a Barrett! But it may not be too late for you yet. I'm an old sea dog now, with one paw in the grave and I'm setting out this very night on my last voyage. Before I go, I want you to know that I've left everything to you – my cottage, my boat and the few savings I've put by over the years. But you must promise me something in return.'

'What is is, great uncle?'

Old Obadiah's eyes blazed like St Elmo's fire.

'Give up pea-counting, come to live in this cottage and *do* something with your life!'

And so it was that William Barrett resigned from the Royal Pea-Counting Service and moved into his great uncle's cottage at the far end of Littlewick Bay with his cat, Polly. He whitewashed the walls, planted lavender in the garden, grew roses around the door and tried to work out how he could keep the promise he had made old Obadiah.

Deciding that it would be better to keep his past life a secret, William packed away his green Pea-Counter's uniform and wore one of Obadiah's old sea captain's jackets instead. Whenever anyone asked him what he had

done before he moved to Littlewick, he winked
and said 'Ha-har!' in such a mysterious and
nautical fashion that people jumped to the
wrong conclusion and assumed he was a
retired pirate. William did nothing to correct
them – being mistaken for a pirate made him
feel rather daring and he was sure that Great
Uncle Obadiah would have approved.

Two: Find the sign of the 'Unsavoury Sheep'

Close by the Littlewick harbour stood a tavern called 'The Unsavoury Sheep'. It was run by Miss Constance, a small mountain of a woman. Three regular customers at the tavern really *were* retired pirates. There was Peg-Leg Jenkins, who had lost his left leg below the knee (a barracuda bit it off); Black Patch Nathan, who had lost one eye (in a knife-fight); and Taffy Thomas, who had managed to be a pirate for thirty years without losing anything. Successful pirates made their way up in the world and retired to sunny South Sea islands, but Peg-Leg, Black Patch and Taffy were so bungling that Littlewick had been the best they could manage.

One rainy night, the three old salts gathered around their favourite table in the tap room and ordered a bottle of grog. When their tumblers were brimming, Peg-Leg proposed a toast.

''Ere's to the Good Old Days, me buckoes!'

The pirates drained their glasses and smacked their lips.

'Ah!' sighed Taffy. 'There's different the grog tastes, nowadays!'

'Too right, mate,' agreed Black Patch. 'They don't make grog like they used to in the Good Old Days.'

'Aye!' nodded Peg-Leg. 'In the Good Old Days, the grog tasted somethin' shockin'!'

'Like shark's bile mixed with cod-liver oil!' said Taffy, pulling a face at the memory.

Peg-Leg wiped some drops of grog from his grizzled beard. 'Thirty-five years I sailed the seas,' he grumbled. 'I visited the Four Corners of the Earth and – '

'The Earth's round now,' chipped in Taffy. 'It ain't got no corners no more, see.'

'Taffy,' growled Peg-Leg, 'I'm a-broodin'! I 'ates a man 'oo interrupts me when I'm a– broodin'!'

'Sorry, Peg-Leg!'

'Thirty-five years a-piratin', man and boy,' continued Peg-Leg. 'And what've I got to show for it, eh? Tell me that!'

'There's your peg-leg,' said Black Patch helpfully.

13

Peg-Leg fixed Black Patch with a glare that would have knocked a cat off a wall.

'If you don't mind that tongue o' yourn, old shipmate,' he hissed, 'I'll slit your gizzard!'

'Sorry, Peg-Leg!' whispered Black Patch palely.

'No chests o' gold dubloons, no caskets o' diamond tiaras . . . Why, I never even made a landlubber walk the plank.'

'I did,' said Taffy. 'But I made the feller walk the wrong way along the plank and the other pirates never let me 'ave a go after that, see.'

The pirates' five eyes grew misty for a moment.

"Ere, let's talk about somefin' else, eh?' said

14

Black Patch. 'What d'you reckon to this Royal Weddin' lark, then? I wouldn't mind a butchers at that.'

'What Royal Weddin'?' asked Taffy.

'Princess Janet's gettin' spliced to the Duke o' Bardalino,' explained Black Patch. ''E's sailin' on board the galleon "Vera Cruz" an' it's gonna dock right 'ere in Littlewick! Cor, bet that ship'll be stuffed to the gunwales wiv treasure, eh, Peg-Leg? Er . . . Peg-Leg?'

Peg-Leg seemed not to hear. His mouth was open, his eyes were staring and his beard was bristling with excitement.

'Pieces of eight!' he muttered hoarsely.

'Touch of the collywobbles, is it?' asked Taffy.

'Avast!' cried Peg-Leg. He sprang to his foot, lost his balance and fell over.

The others helped him quickly back into his chair.

'Listen, mates!' he whispered. 'Your talk of a treasure galleon 'as set my mind to workin' in a lawless and piratical manner! 'Tis fate 'as sent this ship our way! It be our last chance!'

'I get what you mean,' said Black Patch thoughtfully.

'Well I don't!' complained Taffy. 'D'you mean we're goin' down to the quayside to cheer and throw confetti? I like a nice weddin'!'

'Neptune give me strength!' groaned Peg-Leg. 'I'm a-talkin' about treasure, man! I'm a-talkin' about seizin' the riches that 'ave slipped through our fingers all these years! I says as 'ow we should set sail, meet that ship . . . and take 'er! Now, who's with me?'

And with that he drew a dagger from his belt and slammed it into the table top, where it stuck quivering.

'Ay-ay!' roared Black Patch.

'Count me in!' cried Taffy.

And they banged their daggers into the table beside Peg-Leg's.

'Oi!' came a shout from behind.

The pirates turned to face Miss Constance.

'Just what do you three old vandals think

you're up to, carvin' up my nice clean table?'

'We be pirates, woman!' snapped Peg-Leg. 'Stickin' knives into tavern tables is pirates' business! Don't you go a-pokin' your long nose into what don't concern you!'

Miss Constance's eyes flashed fire. She cleared the bar in a single vault, landing with a thud that made the room shake. Rolling up her sleeves to reveal a mermaid tatooed on her left forearm, she advanced on the pirates.

'E-e-r, o' course, we'll pay for any damage!' said Peg-Leg quickly.

The fire in Miss Constance's eyes went out. She returned to her place behind the bar and the pirates heaved a sigh of relief.

'It's a dead good idea about the galleon, Peg-Leg,' mused Black Patch, 'but there's one small snag.'

'Snag?' barked Peg-Leg. 'I tell 'ee there's no snag! 'Tis a plan both cunnin' an' bold!'

'Well, I reckon it'd work a bit better if we 'ad a ship we could sail in.'

'Thunder!' cursed Peg-Leg. 'Foiled by a finicky detail!'

'Just a minute!' exclaimed Taffy. 'I've 'eard about another pirate livin' in Littlewick. A real rogue, by all accounts. There's a boat they say he's got, isn't it?'

'What be 'is name?' demanded Peg-Leg. 'Be it me old 'earty, Tidal Wave Flynn?'

'No.'

'It ain't Mad Jock McTaggert, is it?' asked Black Patch.

'No,' said Taffy, ''is name's William Barrett.'

'William Barrett?' hooted Black Patch. 'What sort o' name's that for a pirate?'

'Well ... p'r'aps 'e likes to be called Bill,'

18

suggested Taffy.

'I reckon as 'ow we should pay a little call on Bill Barrett,' said Peg-Leg, 'and check the set of 'is jib!'

Three: Travel north to the Royal Palace

What Black Patch had said about a Royal Wedding was quite true: King Garry and Queen Dawn had announced that their only child, Princess Janet, was to be married to the Duke of Bardalino in the Cathedral of Featherhatch at the end of August.

To tell the truth, the Duke was not exactly the husband the King and Queen had dreamed their daughter might marry, but the Kingdom of Dunroamin was poor, the Duke was terribly rich, and all the loyal Dunroamians were excited at the idea of a Royal Wedding.

Princess Janet was far from thrilled at the prospect of marrying the Duke. In fact, she was angry about it. She boiled over breakfast, grew dour at dinner and seethed through supper, until she couldn't keep her feelings hidden a moment longer.

She burst into her parents' bedchamber,

interrupting their night-time cocoa.

'It's no good!' she announced. 'I just can't go through with this awful marriage!'

'Why ever not?' asked the King, dismayed.

'Because I can't stand the Duke of Barda-lino!' replied the Princess. 'He's fat!'

'Try to think of him as being a fine figure of a man,' advised Queen Dawn.

'He's also ugly, greedy, his table manners are revolting, he wears the most ridiculous clothes and he suffers from wind!'

'Love can take time to grow, dear,' said the Queen.

'Oh why can't I marry someone else?' cried the Princess desperately.

'We must face facts, Janet,' said the King. 'Things aren't going too well in the realm. In Bardalino, the National Costume is silk and lace. Here, it's sacks.'

'And what's wrong with sacks?' demanded the Princess.

'They're rather common, you must admit,' said the King. 'And I don't know what the Duke's going to think of Featherhatch Cath-edral. The Cathedral of Bardalino is built of solid pink marble.'

'I like Featherhatch Cathedral!' retorted the

Princess hotly. 'Corrugated iron is very practical, and the roof's only a little bit rusty. You're such a snob, Father.'

'You can't criticise me for that, Janet,' said King Garry. 'It says in my Rule Book that it's quite fashionable for monarchs to be a bit snobby, otherwise there's no point in having them. Anyway, the final straw came last week when we were burgled.'

'Burgled?' gasped Princess Janet. 'What was stolen?'

'Nothing,' admitted the King. 'That's the point! The burglars left some money behind with a note to say that they hoped things would take a turn for the better in future. It was most humiliating!'

Princess Janet stamped her foot.

'Money, money, money!' she shouted. 'That's all you ever think about. Money can't buy you happiness, you know!'

'True,' observed the Queen, 'but with money at least one can be miserable in comfort.'

'But I'm not miserable,' cried the Princess. 'I'm perfectly happy just as I am!'

And she burst into tears.

The King and Queen regarded one another sadly.

'She's quite right, you know,' said King Garry. 'The Duke of Bardalino is absolutely repulsive!'

'If only his money wasn't so handsome!' sighed Queen Dawn. 'It's a shame we can't think of a way of getting our hands on his wealth without having to marry him to our Janet.'

The Princess stopped crying when she heard this, and her eyes went all thoughtful.

'Daddykins!' she said sweetly. 'Doesn't the Lord Chancellor have a big book that has all the names and addresses of the wickedest people in the kingdom written down in it?'

'Yes, my dear. Why?'

'There isn't a section on pirates in it, is there?'

'I believe there is,' said the King. 'But why are you interested in pirates?'

'A sudden whim,' explained the Princess. 'It says in my Rule Book that it's very fashionable for Princesses to have sudden whims!'

Four: Sail south to Bardalino

To tell the truth again, Princess Janet was not the only person who was reluctant about the marriage. The Duke of Bardalino himself was having second thoughts. He confided his doubts to his Prime Minister one morning as he browsed through designs for a sailing outfit.

'You know, Pepe,' he said, 'I'm beginning to wonder if getting married is such a good idea.'

'Really, your Grace?'

The Duke gestured towards the full-length portrait of Princess Janet that hung on the wall of his private apartment.

'She's a bit on the skinny side, isn't she?'

'A little . . . slender, perhaps,' said the Prime Minister tactfully.

'I prefer women who are plump,' frowned the Duke. 'Take the Countess of Classico, for instance. Twenty stone if she's an ounce! She's more my type!'

'Unfortunately, the Countess is already married, your Grace,' said the Prime Minister, 'and there is no denying the fact that Princess Janet is quite dazzlingly beautiful!'

'And that's another thing!' said the Duke petulantly. 'She's *so* beautiful that everyone will keep staring at her and I shall be completely ignored!'

The Prime Minister stepped back and took a long look at the Duke. He was wearing a sky-blue satin coat, breeches trimmed with silver lace and a frilly yellow silk shirt.

'Your Grace need have no fears about being

overlooked,' he announced confidently.

At that moment, a page appeared.

'Captain Roderigo, your Grace,' he proclaimed, bowing low.

He bowed rather too low, for when Captain Roderigo appeared, carrying a large pile of rolled-up charts, he fell over the page, scattering the charts far and wide.

By the time he had gathered everything together again, Captain Roderigo was blushing furiously.

'Your Grease – I mean, your Grace,' he said, bowing and dropping two charts. 'I have come to outline the exact course of your Nuptial Voyage to see if it meets with your approval.'

'You shouldn't have bothered!' said the Duke. 'It sounds extremely boring. All I want to know is, will there be any nice scenery on the way?'

'Scenery, your Grace?' frowned Captain Roderigo.

'Yes! What will there be to look at on this voyage?' snapped the Duke.

'Er, the sea, your Grace.'

'I don't like the sea!' exclaimed the Duke. 'It's big and wet and it keeps moving about all the time! Make sure I have a nice big mirror in my cabin so I can admire myself when I get bored.'

'It shall be done, your Grace,' said Captain Roderigo, bowing again and dropping four charts.

'What really worries me,' the Duke confided, 'is that I might be attacked by pirates. Tell me, Captain, do you know of any pirates who are planning to attack me?'

'Er, no, your Grace. One of the problems with pirates is that they don't give out any information about their plots in advance.'

'But that's sneaky!' cried the Duke.

'Pirates tend to be a little on the sneaky side, your Grace.'

'Disgusting!' retorted the Duke. 'When I get back, Pepe, remind me to declare piracy illegal!'

'I believe it already is, your Grace,' said the Prime Minister.

Captain Roderigo gave a little sigh – he was not looking forward one little bit to spending three days on the same galleon as the Duke.

Five: Return to the old Admiral's cottage, Littlewick

That very morning, back in Littlewick, William Barrett was out in his front garden trying to do something about the greenfly on his roses. He didn't have the heart to poison or drown the little creatures, so each morning he spent an hour talking to them, trying to persuade them that they would do far better in someone else's garden. Polly the cat found this intriguing and always clambered up on to William's shoulder for a closer look.

When Peg-Leg and the other pirates rounded the corner and saw a man in a sea-captain's coat with a cat on one shoulder, seemingly busy talking to his roses, they were dumbfounded.

'Er ... Taffy,' croaked Peg-Leg, 'be that 'im?'

'That's the feller, right enough,' said Taffy.

'Are you sure 'e be a rough old salt?'

'The scum of the Seven Seas,' said Taffy

confidently.

'But 'e's talkin' to flowers!' burst out Black Patch.

'Stow it, matey!' commanded Peg-Leg. 'You leave the parley to me.'

Peg-Leg stumped over to the garden gate and rasped out, 'Ahoy there, shipmate!'

The unexpected shock of Peg-Leg's greeting made William leap a foot into the air.

'There's lightning reflexes, isn't it?' whispered Taffy to Black Patch.

'Be you Bill Barrett?' asked Peg-Leg, with the terrible leer he imagined was a friendly grin.

Though William had led a quiet life, it did not take long for him to recognise that the

three villainous-looking characters staring intently at him were pirates. The fact that two of them had bits missing suggested they were desperate men and that he had better do nothing to offend them.

'Ah... um... yo ho ho, Captain!' he babbled.

'There be talk around this town that you be one of us, shipmate!'

'One of, er, you?' frowned William.

'Aye!' nodded Peg-Leg, rolling his eyes. 'A rough, gruff pirate bold 'oo calls no man master and spits in the face o' danger!'

'Me?' squeaked William. 'Er, that is – shiver me timbers, messmate!'

Peg-Leg reached inside his coat and brought out a bottle.

'Permission to come aboard and split some grog, matey. There's a little matter o' skullduggery as we'd like to talk over with you.'

William glanced at the pirates' daggers, pistols and cutlasses and said, 'Haul away, boys! Hooray and up she rises!'

As the other pirates made themselves comfortable in the kitchen of the neat little cottage, Peg-Leg drew William to one side.

'Tell me, 'earty, if it ain't too personal a matter, why be you a-carryin' a cat around on your shoulder?'

'Ah, well, I used to have a parrot, you see,' gabbled William, 'but its squawking gave me a headache. Cats are much quieter!'

Glasses were found, the grog was drunk and Peg-Leg set out his plan. William, who was not used to drinking anything stronger than rose-hip tea, began to feel light-headed and strangely excited by Peg-Leg's words.

34

'So,' said Peg-Leg finally, 'be you with us, Bill?'

William trembled. Could this be the chance he had been waiting for, the chance to be a man of derring-do and live up to the Barrett family name at last? He remembered the voice of great uncle Obadiah: '*Do* something with your life!'

'I . . .' he faltered, 'I . . .'

'Ay-ay!' roared the pirates, banging their glasses on the table.

'Oath!' called Taffy. 'Let's swear a bindin' oath!'

Peg-Leg's face darkened into deadly seriousness.

'If any man 'ere should turn yellow-livered,' he rumbled, 'or go a-blabbin' our plan to any-one . . . it'll be the marlinspike for 'im!'

'The marlinspike?' quailed Black Patch. 'Couldn't we make it the same as usual – bein' cut up in little bits an' fed to the sharks?'

'Not when treasure's at stake!' hissed Peg-Leg. 'The sight o' gold does strange things to a man, an' it wouldn't do to be too soft!'

'Ha-har!' agreed the pirates.

'Now then, Bill,' said Peg-Leg briskly, 'tell us about this ship o' yourn?'

'Ship?' asked William.

'Ar! Be it a Barbary Schooner with two gun decks, kitted out wi' racin' sails?'

'Not really.'

'Well, then,' said Peg-Leg, leaning back in his chair, 'belike 'tis a Genoese man o' war, stripped down for speed and stealth!'

'Not exactly,' gulped William.

'What manner o' vessel be it, then?'

'Well,' said William, 'I suppose I'd describe it as being more like a cockle boat sort of thing.'

There was a hard, cold silence.

'A cockle boat?' whispered Peg-Leg.

'Yes,' nodded William, 'you know, the kind of boat people use when they go cockle fishing.'

There was a harder, colder silence.

'Peg-Leg,' said Black Patch in a strangled voice, 'the Duke o' Bardalino'll be in a four-masted, seventy-gun galleon wiv a company o' crack shot marines aboard. An' we'll be in a cockle boat!'

'Steady, man!' ordered Peg-Leg. 'Lady Luck be cruel at times, but we must play the cards as they lie!'

'Um, look,' said William. 'I know we're all rough, gruff pirates bold who spit in the face of danger and all that, but don't you think it would be sensible to change our plans?'

'Change our plans?' wheezed Peg-Leg. 'In what way change our plans?'

'In a forgetting-the-whole-idea sort of way,' suggested William.

This did not go down well with the pirates. They began to mumble and gnash their teeth.

''Ere, mate,' whispered Black Patch to William. 'Cop a whack o' that!' He drew a wickedly pointed hook from his pocket.

'Gracious! Whatever is it?'

'That's a marlinspike,' explained Black Patch.

'Of course,' said William, quickly changing his mind, 'we'll have surprise on our side! No

one would be expecting an attack from a cockle boat, would they?'

'Ha-har!' chorused the pirates.

Six: Thence to the harbour

Peg-Leg, Black Patch and Taffy had seen all sorts of ships in their time at sea, but never before had any of them clapped eyes on the likes of the cockle boat 'Daisy May' as she bobbed in the sparkling waters of Littlewick Bay. She was a short, dumpy boat, covered in bumps and scrapes and her sail was more patch than canvas.

'Be that all of 'er?' asked Peg-Leg. 'You ain't got no extra bits of 'er stored away, by any chance?'

'I'm afraid not,' said William.

'Then there's work to be done, lads!'

Leaks were plugged, woodwork was painted and brass bits were polished up. In a solemn ceremony, the cockle boat was re-named 'Rumguts' and then the pirates went back on to the quayside to survey their handiwork.

'She looks like a floatin' fryin'-pan!' sighed

Peg-Leg.

'Crew!' barked Peg-Leg rallying his men. 'The day after tomorrow, the "Vera Cruz" be due in these waters. I suggest as we should adjourn to "The Unsavoury Sheep" to pore over our sea-charts, discuss our plan of attack and get roarin' drunk. What say 'ee?'

'Ha-har!' shouted Black Patch and Taffy.

'Um, oh, all right then,' muttered William.

Seven: Beware seagulls . . .

Aboard the galleon 'Vera Cruz', the Duke of Bardalino was up on the main deck, nervously scouring the horizon with his special gold telescope. He was dressed in a pink satin suit, trimmed with lime green lace and a matching three-cornered hat festooned with yellow ostrich plumes.

"E looks like a trifle!' commented one of the sailors.

'I pity that poor Princess, marryin' that cowardly lump!' grumbled his mate.

Suddenly, the Duke went quite red and started jumping up and down.

'Pirates!' he squealed. 'Pirates! Quick, quick! Open fire!'

Within a few seconds, cannon were pounding on all sides and the marines' muskets were crackling.

Captain Roderigo stumbled over to the

42

Duke, coughing his way through thick clouds of gunpowder smoke.

'Where are the pirates, your Grace?' he enquired above the booming and banging.

'Over there!' waved the Duke.

Captain Roderigo held his telescope to his eye.

'Your Grace, I can see nothing but a flock of seagulls.'

'They look suspicious to me!' shrieked the Duke. 'They could fly on board at night and murder us in our hammocks!'

'Cease fire!' ordered the Captain. When the din had died down, he addressed the Duke with as much tact as he could manage.

'Although it's not my place to criticise, your Grace, I must point out that since we began our voyage, you've ordered us to sink our escort ships, blow two fishing smacks to smithereens and badly frighten a school of whales.'

'Only trying to protect myself!' said the Duke haughtily and he flounced off below decks.

'That poor, poor Princess!' whispered Captain Roderigo.

Eight: ... and masked strangers

In Littlewick, events were taking a most unexpected turn. When the pirates arrived at the tavern, Miss Constance told them a visitor was waiting for them in an upstairs chamber.

The mysterious visitor did not believe in taking chances. All the curtains in the room were tightly drawn and its occupant was wearing a hooded cloak – hood pulled well down over the face – as well as a mask. The voice that emerged from the mask was well-spoken, young and female.

'Gentlemen, I have good reason to believe that you all are, or once were, pirates. Is that true?'

'Madam,' said Peg-Leg proudly, 'we are as low a pack of bilge-rats as ever crawled a quarter-deck!'

'Time is short and I must speak frankly,' said the young woman. 'I need the services of a band of desperate men who fear nothing. The day after tomorrow, the "Vera Cruz" is due to dock with the Duke of Bardalino on board.'

'Really?' cried Peg-Leg in exaggerated surprise. 'Well, well, lads, who'd 'ave thought it!'

'That ship will never arrive at Littlewick,' said the stranger grimly, 'if you help me sink her! My plan is this. We'll board the "Vera Cruz" at night, pretending to be the pilot come to guide the galleon safely into harbour. But instead of doing that, we'll sail due west and run her on to Dragon Reef. We'll help ourselves to treasure while the crew and passengers are manning the lifeboats.'

Peg-Leg's eyes were glazed with admiration. ''Tis brilliant!' he breathed. 'It can only 'ave been thought up by someone with a devious, low-down, cunnin' nature. I like that in a woman! Welcome aboard, matess!'

'Er, Peg-Leg,' whispered Taffy, 'are you sure the "Rumguts" will 'old us all?'

'What be the matter wi' you?' sneered Peg-Leg. 'Lost your belly for adventure?'

'I like adventure, all right,' explained Taffy, 'it's just drownin' I'm not too keen on, see!'

'Madam,' Peg-Leg announced, 'we'll meet you in this tavern just afore midnight tomorrow

47

night! And now, crew, let's adjourn to the tap-room to toast our success!'

Peg-Leg, Black Patch and Taffy filed out, laughing and chattering. William, however, lingered and when the last pirate had left the room, he closed the door and bowed low to the stranger.

'Your Highness!' he said humbly.

'Highness? What do you mean?'

'Forgive me, ma'am,' said William. 'You see, I'm not really a pirate at all. I used to be Royal Pea-Counter-in-Chief and I met you once or twice. As soon as you spoke, I recognised you ... Princess Janet!'

'Botheration!' sighed the Princess, removing her mask. 'I thought you looked familiar. You didn't look as piratical as the others, and the cat on your shoulder made you stand out. I suppose I've got no choice now but to explain the whole sorry business to you ...'

And Princess Janet told William all about herself and her desperate plan to get her hands on enough treasure to avoid having to marry the Duke of Bardalino.

As she spoke, William trembled. He seemed to hear again the voice of great uncle Obadiah, '*Do* something with your life!' And he felt sure that this really was his chance to be a man of derring-do and live up to the Barrett family name.

'Your Highness,' he said when the Princess had finished, 'rest assured I shall keep your true identity a secret and do all in my power to ensure that this marriage never takes place!'

Nine: Set sail at night

The following night, just after midnight, the 'Rumguts' sailed stealthily out of Littlewick Harbour.

Or, perhaps 'stealthily' is not quite the right word, because there was a certain amount of rowing around in circles and bumping into other boats in the dark. But before long, the gallant little boat and her daring crew were out on the open sea.

Conditions on board were rather uncomfortable. There was only room for one person to sit down and that was Black Patch, who was steering. Peg-Leg stood at the prow of the boat, waving his cutlass. Taffy, William and Princess Janet stood in the middle, where they were clonked by the sail every time the wind changed direction.

Black Patch took a deep lungful of sea air and breathed it out in a long sigh.

'There's nuffin' like this!' he announced. 'Every time I goes back to sea after a spell ashore, I asks meself the same question – why the 'ell can't I tell when I'm well off?'

Princess Janet seemed in high spirits.

'Isn't this exciting, William?' she whispered.

'In a terrifying way, your Highness.'

'I've never seen a cat on a sea voyage

before. Does Polly like sailing?'

'I'm not sure, your Highness,' replied William. 'But she is fond of fish.'

William was not sure if he liked sailing himself, especially on an undeniably small and overcrowded boat.

'I can feel water on my feet!' he shouted.

'Nothin' to worry about, boyo!' answered Taffy. 'All boats ship a bit of water.'

'Lights!' yelled Peg-Leg. 'Lights off the starboard bow! 'Tis the "Vera Cruz"! Ar, the very sight of 'er do make the blood quicken in me rascally veins!'

'I know I shouldn't feel worried if I feel water on my feet,' said William, 'but is it all right to be a bit concerned if I feel it around my knees?'

'Tarnation!' cursed Peg-Leg. 'Start bailin' for all you're worth! I'll attract the "Vera Cruz" with the signallin' lantern!'

Ten: Make your rendezvous

Up on the main deck of the 'Vera Cruz', a sharp-eyed member of the watch spotted the urgent signalling of a light and conveyed its message to Captain Roderigo.

'Boat claiming to be the Littlewick pilot off the port bow, sir. It says it's in difficulties and would we come alongside.'

Captain Roderigo narrowed his eyes suspiciously. 'Two degrees to port helmsman!' he barked. 'Er... it *is* port, isn't it?'

'Ay-ay, sir! You think it might be an ambush?'

'I'm not sure,' said Captain Roderigo. 'But whatever you do, don't tell the Duke. If it's pirates, we can take care of ourselves. If it's not pirates and the Duke hears about it, those poor devils won't stand a chance!'

It turned out to be more like a rescue than a pirate ambush. By the time the galleon arrived, the 'Rumguts' had all but sunk and its crew was thoroughly cold, wet and miserable. When they clambered aboard the 'Vera Cruz' and found themselves surrounded by armed marines, they knew the game was up.

'I should have known something like this would happen!' wailed William. 'I just wasn't cut out for a life of crime.'

'Never say die, boyo,' whispered Taffy encouragingly.

'Why not?' asked William. 'They're going to hang us, aren't they?'

'On the spot. They'll draw and quarter us, too, if they know their business, see.'

The pirates and the masked Princess were lined up and Captain Roderigo inspected them by the light of a storm lantern.

'You,' he told Peg-Leg, 'have got the shiftiest, most villainous and untrustworthy face I've ever seen.'

'Thankee, Cap'n, you're a real toff!' beamed Peg-Leg.

The Captain gave Taffy and Black Patch no more than a scornful glance, but when he came to William, his face opened wide with astonishment.

'You look nothing like a pirate to me! You

55

look more like a Pea-Counter! And what's that cat doing on your head?'

'Well,' William explained, 'she was on my shoulder, but when the boat started to sink she tried to get as far away from the water as possible.'

The Captain moved on to the masked figure with downcast eyes at the end of the line and his face closed into a troubled frown.

'And as for you, you scruffy little sea-vixen . . .' he began.

'Scruffy little sea-vixen?' gasped the offended Princess, gazing straight at the captain. Then she gulped and chuntered, 'Um ... er ... well ... I ...' for the sight of Captain Roderigo's dashingly handsome face had set her heart all a-flutter.

'Er ... I demand to see the Duke of Bardalino!' she managed at last.

'The Duke?' muttered Captain Roderigo. 'But how do you know that ... ?' At that moment, the cord holding Princess Janet's mask went ping and the mask went clattering on to the deck.

'Um ... er ... well ... I ...' chuntered Captain Roderigo, for the sight of Princess Janet's peerless beauty had set *his* heart all a-flutter.

'Er ... Sergeant of Marines,' he said, not taking his eyes from the Princess's face. 'Slip down to the Duke's quarters and tell him to come on deck at once.'

'Ay-ay, sir!'

In a matter of moments, the Duke of Bardalino bustled on deck, wearing scarlet pyjamas with gold fringing and a lilac nightcap.

'How dare you wake me at this unholy hour, Captain Roderigo!' he blustered. 'Who are all these nasty wet people and – Santa Domenigo!

Princess Janet! What are you doing here?'

The Princess bore down on the Duke with a face like thunder.

'I've come to tell you I think you're a big, fat slug and I wouldn't marry you if you were the last man on earth! As far as I'm concerned you can go straight back to Bardalino this minute, and if I never see your wobbly, piggy-eyed face again, it'll be too soon for me!'

The crew, who had all left their posts to watch the excitement, gave the Princess a round of applause. When it had died down, the Duke stammered, 'B-but, does this mean our wedding is off?'

As he spoke, William Barrett trembled. He had an idea that he was absolutely *certain* was derring-doish and worthy of the name 'Barrett'.

'A moment, if you please!' he called out. All eyes turned on him.

'Captain Roderigo, are you, by any chance, a rich man?'

'Quite well off,' replied the Captain. 'As a matter of fact, this is my last voyage. I'm leaving the navy to start a silkworm ranch in the West Indies.'

'And are you married at all?' asked William.

'Not even slightly,' replied the Captain. 'I never met a lady I wished to marry...' he turned to the Princess, '... until this very moment!'

'Ooh!' sighed Princess Janet.

'Ooh!' sighed Captain Roderigo.

'And you, sir,' William said to the Duke. 'Now you know Princess Janet's true feelings, I trust you'll do the gentlemanly thing and call off the wedding?'

'I'm no spoil-sport!' said the Duke. 'Roderigo's more than welcome to her. She's got a tongue like a fish-wife!'

'Very well, then!' cried William. 'Three cheers for Captain Roderigo and Princess Janet!'

They only got as far as the second cheer: with all the crew eagerly watching the action on deck, the 'Vera Cruz' had been drifting unattended for some time.

She ran straight on to Dragon Reef.

Eleven: Treasure for all!

So it was that the pirates bold and Princess Janet found themselves sinking for the second time in the same night. Fortunately, the galleon's crew was so well-trained that everybody was in the lifeboats before there was any real danger.

King Garry and Queen Dawn were delighted when they heard the news and gave their consent to the marriage of Princess Janet and Captain Roderigo at once. The happy couple settled in the West Indies and the silken thread from their ranch was shipped back to Featherhatch to be woven into fine garments that were sold in other countries. Before many years had passed, King Garry and Queen Dawn's realm had grown so prosperous that all their subjects had enough of what they wanted.

The Duke of Bardalino caught a chill on the

night of the wreck and took up temporary residence in 'The Unsavoury Sheep', where Miss Constance took such good care of him that he lost his heart and promptly married her.

William Barrett, certain that old Obadiah would be proud of him at last, took Polly back to his trim little whitewashed cottage and hoped that he would have nothing to do with pirates ever again.

But one stormy night, he answered an

urgent knocking on his door to find Peg-Leg, Black Patch and Taffy gathered on the front step.

'Avast there, me old shipmate!' cried Peg-Leg. 'The lads and I 'ave come up with a bit of an idea, like, an' we was a-wonderin' if you might be interested.'

'An idea?' squeaked William apprehensively.

'Ar! 'Tis about salvagin' sunken treasure from the wreck o' the galleon "Vera Cruz" . . .' Peg-Leg winked and held up a bottle. 'What

say we discuss the matter over a few glasses o' grog?'

'Ha-har!' bawled Black Patch and Taffy.